To ?

CW00853243

The Adventures of
Sleepy The Magical Bear

Best Wishes

D. M. Russell

© D M Rivers, 2012

Published by D M Rivers

The rights of D M Rivers to be identified as the author of this work have been asserted in accordance with the Copyright, Designs and Patents Act 1988.

A CIP catalogue record for this book is available from the British Library.

ISBN 978-0-9574787-0-1

Book and cover design by Clare Brayshaw

Prepared and printed by:

York Publishing Services Ltd
64 Hallfield Road
Layerthorpe
York YO31 7ZQ

Tel: 01904 431213

Website: www.yps-publishing.co.uk

www.sleepymagic.co.uk

The Adventures of Sleepy The Magical Bear

D.M. Rivers

D.M. RIVERS

Illustrated by Margaret Ellis A.T.D.

Chapter 1

A Visit to the Shops

The Onion family were an ordinary family who lived in a small town in southern England called Tupstall. The father, Harold, was a teacher of sciences, and Mary, the mother, worked as a bank clerk. Then there was Jenny, their young daughter, who was a fun, outgoing girl with mousey-brown hair and she always wore a pleasant, happy smile.

Easter was fast approaching and it was time for Jenny and her parents to do some shopping, so one rainy Saturday morning the family visited Tupstall Shopping Centre. They were busy browsing the vast array of shops, when Jenny saw one with a "Just Opened" sign displayed in its front window.

'Mummy, why don't we go in here; this place looks amazing,' said Jenny.

'OK then, Jenny. Let's see what's inside,' said her mummy.

The shop was full of soft toys, train sets and rocking horses.

'Wow! I'm glad we came in here,' beamed Jenny.

Jenny looked at all the shelves piled high with soft toys until she saw a bear all on his own. He was wearing a purple nightgown and purple nightcap. To Jenny's amazement, the bear lifted his right paw and began waving at Jenny. To Jenny, time stood still. Eventually, she summoned the courage to wave back at the bear, wondering if her eyes had seen right.

'OK, let's go, Jenny, there are still more shops to see. We can come back tomorrow,' said her mother.

Jenny moaned, 'But, Mum, I want to stay here.'

'Not now, Jenny. Come on, do as you're told.'

Jenny waved goodbye to the bear and the bear waved back at Jenny.

That night, Jenny could not sleep. Instead, she counted the hours until she could go back to the new shop. Whatever happened, she was determined to return to see the bear who waved at her.

Sunshine greeted the town of Tupstall the next day and the first thing Jenny asked her mother was if she could go back to the same shop as the day before.

'OK,' her mum agreed. 'Let's go, Jenny. You're in luck; I need to buy your uncle an Easter present.'

Jenny ran downstairs to put her coat on and off they went to town.

As they approached Tupstall Shopping Centre Jenny said, 'Please, Mummy, can we go to the new shop first?'

'OK, then,' her mother agreed. 'Perhaps we can buy you something for Easter, too.'

Jenny had only one thing on her mind and that was to find the same bear she had seen the day before. When they arrived at the shop there it was, right in front of Jenny, sitting on the same shelf as before with its fur glistening like a golden fleece. Jenny waved at the bear, who again waved back at Jenny.

'That's it, Mum. This is what I want for Easter, please,' said Jenny to her mum.

'What, another bear, Jenny? You have three bears already, why do you need another one?'

'But, Mummy, none of the others are like this one. Please, please can you buy me this bear?' she pleaded.

'Well OK, Jenny, as you've been so good I'll buy it for you,' said her mother.

Jenny broke out in a huge smile as she held her bear for the first time. The bear had the most beautiful smile. Its fur was warm and it had the most captivating, magical dark brown eyes she had ever seen. Jenny held her new bear close to her as her mum finished the shopping.

Just then, Jenny saw the bear wink and she looked in amazement at what had just happened …

Chapter 2

Sleepy Magic

As soon as Jenny got home she raced upstairs to her bedroom clutching her new bear.

'OK. Now first of all I need a name for you. With such a beautiful nightgown and nightcap, I think I'll have to call you Sleepy,' said Jenny.

Instantly, the bear said, 'Hi. Thank you so much for choosing me. The name you have given to me happens to be the name where I come from.'

Jenny could not believe it.

'Sleepy, you can talk!'

'Yes,' said Sleepy. 'I have many magical powers and I shall share them with you, Jenny.'

Just then, Sleepy waved his right paw and his nightgown turned from purple to yellow and the nightcap was now a yellow sports cap. A moment later, Sleepy changed back to his original purple nightgown.

'That is amazing, Sleepy. It saves buying clothes,' said Jenny.

'Yes, it is, isn't it. I can change my clothes at any time,' said Sleepy. 'Tell me, Jenny. Why did you choose me amongst so many other toys?'

'I felt something magical when I looked at you, Sleepy,' said Jenny.

At that moment, Jenny heard her parents approaching her room.

'Who are you talking to?' her mum asked.

Jenny replied, 'I'm talking to Sleepy, my bear. We're chatting together.'

'Oh! don't be so silly, Jenny,' said her mother, 'bears don't talk. Now wash your hands and come down for dinner.'

'OK, Mum.'

Jenny turned to Sleepy once her mother had left the room and said, 'Sleepy, why don't they understand?'

'Don't worry, Jenny, they will in time,' said Sleepy softly.

After dinner Jenny went to bed and before turning out the light she said goodnight to Sleepy.

'I'm so happy to have you in my life. Will you come with me to school tomorrow?'

'Of course I will; it will be my pleasure, Jenny,' said Sleepy.

Jenny held Sleepy in her arms and she knew happy times lay ahead. She also knew that from now on school would be far more enjoyable, too.

'Sleepy, can you show me some of your magic?' she asked.

'Sure, watch this …' said Sleepy. Sleepy blew three bubbles in the air. Inside each bubble was a turtle, a rabbit and a zebra respectively. 'I have many magical gifts that I want to share with you, Jenny,' said Sleepy.

'What else can you do, Sleepy?' asked Jenny, her voice full of excitement.

'Every day you will see and discover a little more Sleepy magic. But all in good time, Jenny, all in good time,' said Sleepy. 'You need to get your head down now.'

Jenny could hear her parents walking up the stairs towards her room.

Mrs Onion said, 'What's all that talking about? It's lights out time, Jenny. You need to go to sleep now; you've got school in the morning, don't forget.'

'It's me and Sleepy, Mum, we're talking.'

'OK, Jenny, now come on, it's time to put Sleepy down,' said her mother. 'And no more of this nonsense.'

'OK, Mum,' said Jenny. 'And thank you for buying Sleepy for me.'

As Mrs Onion left the room Jenny held Sleepy and said, 'Don't worry, Sleepy, I'll never let go of you. I will always be here for you.'

'I think we should celebrate our friendship with a magic lollipop,' he announced. Sleepy waved his paw and a lollipop appeared in all the colours of the rainbow. Each colour was a different flavour. 'There is strawberry, chocolate, vanilla, blueberry … and wait till you get to the raspberry – that's my favourite,' said Sleepy.

'Thanks, Sleepy. Yum-yum. This is the best lollipop I've ever had.'

Sleepy and Jenny then drifted off to sleep.

Chapter 3

School Time

The next morning Jenny woke up early.

'Wake up, Sleepy; it's time for school.'

'I'm looking forward to going to your school,' said Sleepy, 'and meeting all your friends.'

Jenny smiled. 'Me, too. It will be really exciting to have you with me at school. But we had better eat some breakfast first.'

At the breakfast table Sleepy spoke to Jenny.

'My favourite breakfast of sausage and beans coming up. Delicious!'

Sleepy waved his paw and a tin of beans and three sausages floated off the shelf and were suspended in mid-air. Then the tin opened and the beans flew out of the tin and into a saucepan, where they appeared to be cooking. The sausages sizzled away in a frying pan, right next to Mrs Onion, who did not appear to see or smell a thing. Once cooked, the food transferred itself onto a plate and landed in front of Sleepy and Jenny.

'This tastes great,' Sleepy said to Jenny, who just looked in shock at what had just happened, almost disbelieving.

After breakfast, Mr Onion said, 'OK, Jenny, let's go. I'll drive you to school today but you will have to get the school bus back as I'm going to be late home.'

'OK, Dad,' Jenny said. 'See you at dinner tonight, Mum.'

Jenny held Sleepy tightly as she clambered out of her father's car. Then she turned and whispered, 'Here we go, Sleepy. Welcome to Tupstall Primary School.'

On arrival at Jenny's class, three pupils who she did not get on well with were waiting for her. Sarah Pasty, Fiona Staples and Gordon Vase looked directly at her and Sleepy and then giggled together, all huddled in a circle, whispering unkind words to each other.

'Jenny, I can hear children sniggering at you,' said Sleepy, noticing that she had gone quiet.

'Oh, don't worry, Sleepy. They are always doing this. I just pretend they are not there,' replied Jenny.

'Well I don't like to see you upset, Jenny, and I'm going to use a little Sleepy magic on them.'

'That's fine by me,' she said, now a little happier.

Sleepy waved his paws up and down twice and the three pupils turned into a bowl of rhubarb crumble, a plate of sausage and chips, and a cheese sandwich.

'The children will stay like this until home time and then I will change them back to their normal selves,' said Sleepy.

'Thank you, Sleepy. At least I won't have any problems from these three today,' Jenny said happily.

Jenny's first lesson of the day was chemistry. The class was learning how to turn leaves into different colours with the help of dyes, but Jenny was struggling to make her experiment work.

'Please can you help me, Sleepy?' she asked.

Sleepy shook his right leg and the leaves turned into all the colours of the rainbow. Then they began to float in mid-air. Jenny could not believe her eyes. The leaves spelt out the name "Sleepy", suspended in the air. As the leaves floated gently back down on the table, Jenny hugged Sleepy and told her how much she loved him.

'I love you too, Jenny.'

Later that day, when Jenny went back to her class, she noticed that Sarah, Fiona and Gordon were still in the form of plates of food.

'I think it's time you turned them back, Sleepy,' said Jenny.

'OK, if you're sure. Here goes,' said Sleepy and with a wave of his paw, the pupils were back to normal.

They all looked at Jenny with friendship in their eyes for the first time and all three of them apologised to Jenny for laughing at her. Jenny forgave them and winked at Sleepy.

At home time Jenny and Sleepy began to make their way to the school bus stop.

Sleepy nudged Jenny and said, 'Jenny, why get the bus when you can come home in the Sleepster?'

'What's a Sleepster?'

'It's my car from my land. I'll drive you home in it. It's a lot quicker and much more fun than getting the bus.'

'OK, Sleepy, let's go,' said an excited Jenny.

As Jenny walked towards an old oak tree near the school grounds, a gust of wind nearly blew her over. No sooner had she regained her footing than she was amazed to see Sleepy's shiny white car before her with dazzling headlights and the most amazing interior that anyone could dream of.

Jenny opened the front door and Sleepy said, 'Jump in, Jenny.'

The engines on the Sleepster roared like a rocket, ready for take-off. With a *whoosh*! they were gone, zipping through the rush-hour traffic and past the school bus.

'Don't worry, Jenny, no one can see us,' said Sleepy.

'What does this orange button do, Sleepy?' asked Jenny, slowly getting used to her surroundings.

'Well if you press it, your favourite ice cream will come out. Go for it!' said Sleepy.

Jenny pressed the button and a chocolate fudge ice cream with a caramel cone came out of the dashboard with a sprinkle of strawberry chips.

'Yum-yum, Sleepy, this is super delicious,' said Jenny.

'My pleasure. I'm glad you like it,' said Sleepy.

As the Sleepster pulled up outside Jenny's house, Jenny thanked Sleepy for the ride home.

'That's some car you have there, Sleepy. I can't wait to go in it again.'

'Everyone has a Sleepster in my land, Jenny. It's the quickest way to travel.'

'Your land sounds amazing. Can we go there one day, Sleepy? I'd love to see it,' asked Jenny.

'Jenny, I would be more than happy to take you to my home in Magicville.'

As Jenny and Sleepy opened the front door they could smell Jenny's favourite dinner of shepherd's pie and gravy.

'Oooh, that smells delicious, Sleepy. Better not tell Mum I've just had an ice cream.'

'It's our secret, Jenny. Mum's the word. Shepherd's pie here we come,' said Sleepy cheekily.

Chapter 4

A Weekend to Remember

Early the following Saturday morning it was time for the Onion family to head off for a weekend away at the seaside town of Gravy. Jenny and Sleepy climbed into the family car and they headed off for the two-hour drive to Gravy.

'Wish we were in the Sleepster; we would be there by now,' Jenny said to Sleepy after the first ten minutes of their journey.

'This car makes a nice change though, Jenny, and we've only got another hour and fifty minutes to go,' replied Sleepy.

'I know,' replied a glum-looking Jenny.

'Let's play magic bubbles,' said Sleepy.

Sleepy spent the next hour blowing lots of different animal shapes ranging from elephants to camels and Jenny was soon enjoying the car journey.

Eventually, the family arrived at Gravy and the car pulled up outside their holiday cottage.

Jenny unpacked and said, 'Let's go and see my friends Freda and Olive. They will be waiting to see us, Sleepy.'

Olive was 7 years of age and was poorly. She had written a letter to Jenny about her ill health, saying that the doctors didn't know what was wrong with her.

Jenny and Sleepy arrived at Olive's house and knocked on the front door. Mrs Murray, Olive's mother, answered and greeted Jenny with a big hug.

'Olive is upstairs; we're waiting for the doctor to arrive. Please go up. Olive can't wait to see you. Oh! and that's a lovely bear you have there, Jenny.'

Without replying in her haste to see Olive, she raced up the stairs and opened Olive's bedroom door. Her friend looked very poorly, indeed.

'Olive, Olive are you OK?' asked Jenny.

Olive whispered weakly, 'Hi, Jenny. It's great to see you. I'm not sure why I'm so ill. No one knows what's wrong with me. I feel terrible. Awww! I love your bear. What's it called?'

'Oh! thanks,' replied Jenny with tears in her eyes. 'He's called Sleepy.'

Sleepy tapped Jenny on her shoulder and said, 'Let me help her, Jenny.' Sleepy put his right paw on Olive's hand and whispered five words that no one could hear. He then gave Olive a hug. 'Now count to five,' Sleepy told Olive.

'OK,' she agreed, surprised. At first Olive couldn't believe she was talking to a bear, but she counted to five nonetheless. 'One, two, three, four, five...'

Mrs Murray entered the room and she saw Olive standing up and laughing with Jenny.

'I– I– don't believe it! How on earth did you manage to get better, Olive? And so quickly.'

'I'm not sure, but I think Sleepy may have something to do with it.'

Before Mrs Murray could get a full explanation, Olive and Jenny said, 'See you soon; we're off to the beach!'

Mrs Murray looked on in amazement, but they were gone before she could question them further.

Olive Jenny and Sleepy arrived at the beach and met up with Freda, an adventurous, bubbly girl.

'Hey! Jenny, Olive, how's it going? Great to see you. And your bear looks cool, Jenny,' Freda shouted.

'Thanks. Now what shall we do?' Jenny asked Freda.

'Let's go on my uncle's motorboat to the old abandoned ship about a mile out to sea. We can explore it.'

'OK, sounds like a plan. Ready when you are.'

'Give us a few minutes and I'll be right back,' said Freda.

'Ahoy there, sailors,' said Uncle Tom, Freda's uncle, a few minutes later. 'I understand you want to visit the old abandoned ship. I'll take you there, but you will only have about thirty minutes to explore before I pick you up as the tide turns soon.'

Uncle Tom wore a fisherman's cap and a green rain jacket and he looked every inch a fisherman.

They soon arrived at the old abandoned ship. It was old and rickety and swayed gently. There was a mysterious air to it which was rather unnerving. The children and Sleepy began to explore the ship, going from room to room until Freda spotted an old box under a tablecloth.

'Wow! there could be treasure in this,' said Freda excitedly.

'Don't open the box,' Sleepy cautioned Freda.

But it was too late – Freda had already opened the box. Inside was a note which read:

Many a time in this ship's life did it sail free.

Now the box has been opened, sail again we go.

'Freda, this is the Box of Time,' stated Sleepy. 'You should not have opened it. This is not good.'

Just then the ship then started to rock from side to side before heading out into the open waters.

'Can you help, Sleepy?' Jenny asked. 'I don't want to be on here any more. I'm scared.'

'The Box of Time has strong magic surrounding it, Jenny. There is only one way of stopping the ship and that is if I go back to Magicville for a short period of time to bring back the magic code of Tronja. This will unlock the box and stop the ship from sailing any further out,' said Sleepy.

Jenny hugged Sleepy tightly and a tear appeared in her eye. But before she could wipe it away, Sleepy had disappeared.

'Are you OK?' Freda asked Jenny. 'You look upset.'

'I don't like this. I want to go home. And Sleepy – he's gone, Freda. I'm so worried.'

A second later Sleepy reappeared.

'No he hasn't; he's right here.'

'Sorry I'm so late. I now have what we're looking for – the magic code of Tronja.'

The children smiled in relief.

'Wow! that was quick,' said Olive.

'I know; I took the Sleepster. Here is the magic code,' said Sleepy. He tapped on the box five times using the magic code of Tronja and the ship stopped sailing immediately. 'The Box of Time is now closed.'

'Thank you, Sleepy, you are the best,' they chorused.

'You're welcome. I think that's enough exploring and excitement for one day. Listen, I can hear your uncle's boat coming back. It's time to get off the ship,' Sleepy told the treasure hunters.

'Did you have a fun time, kids?' asked Uncle Tom.

'Yes, Uncle Tom. But how did you find us?' asked Freda.

'What do you mean? You are exactly where I dropped you off,' said Uncle Tom.

The children looked puzzled as they had sailed several miles out to sea.

'Oh well, we'll tell you another time, Uncle Tom. We just want to go home now.'

Back on the beach the children all gave Sleepy a hug.

'Now for a quiet evening in,' said Jenny. 'I think we all need a good night's sleep after today's adventure.'

Everybody agreed and the children and Sleepy headed off to their respective homes.

Chapter 5

Afternoon Tea

Back at home in Tupstall at the breakfast table on the Sunday morning, the Onion family were discussing what they were going to do for the day.

'This afternoon we are visiting my brother, your uncle Gordon, and your aunty Hilda,' said Mr Onion.

'Oh no! not Uncle Gordon and Aunty Hilda. Do I have to go, Dad?' Jenny moaned.

'Yes, you do, Jenny. And Uncle Gordon will be watching your behaviour closely, so only speak when spoken to and none of your silly business with Sleepy,' Mr Onion stated clearly.

The morning passed without event with Jenny and Sleepy playing in the garden.

'Jenny, it's time to go to Uncle Gordon's, let's go,' her father shouted. 'Get a wriggle on.'

'Come on, Sleepy, let's get this over with,' said Jenny.

'What are your uncle and aunty like, Jenny?' asked Sleepy.

'Well, Uncle Gordon is an office manager and he has no sense of humour whatsoever. His idea of fun is reading

his staff rotas. He doesn't like children and he is very, very strict.'

'Yikes!' replies Sleepy.

'And Aunty Hilda. Well, she's not as bad but no one can understand her as she talks too quickly and often says things back to front.'

'Hmm,' said Sleepy, 'I'll have to remember that.'

'Now, Sleepy, we both have to behave or we will be in trouble and we don't want that.'

'*Me*? Misbehave?' said Sleepy, giving Jenny a wink.

As the family walked up the path to Uncle Gordon's house they saw a big sign saying "Trespassers will be sent to the Piranha Pond". Jenny knocked on Uncle Gordon's door and Aunty Hilda opened it.

'Hello, how are you? Do you want a glass of cake and a slice of tea?' she said quickly, once again confusing everyone and getting her words all mixed up.

'Ermm, no thanks,' Jenny replied. 'And isn't that a slice of cake and a cup of tea?'

'That's what I said. Now, move along. Chop-chop, we haven't got all day.'

Jenny, Sleepy and her mother followed Aunty Hilda into the living room and there behind a large newspaper was Uncle Gordon, muttering to himself about stock market losses.

He moved the paper to one side and said, 'So you lot have turned up, then. Well, sit down and don't speak until 3.07 p.m. It's now 3.04 p.m.'

Jenny and Sleepy sat down and did not say another word. Just then her father walked into the room.

'Hello, Gordon, how is my favourite brother?' asked Harold.

'Dad, you are not allowed to speak for another three minutes,' said Jenny.

'Don't be silly; that rule just affects you,' replied her father.

'Oh great!' replied Jenny.

'Cakes and tea?' Aunty Hilda asked as she walked in.

'Oh yes, please. I can speak now so I'll have some,' replied Jenny. 'At least I think that's what she meant,' said Jenny.

Aunt Hilda had said it so fast that Jenny couldn't be sure.

'That's a funny-looking cake,' said Sleepy. 'It's full of sponge with no topping and no filling and it's green-looking.'

'Here we go. Tuck in, everyone; it's a new recipe,' said Hilda, smiling, proud of her achievement. 'It's made out of tealeaves and cabbage pie.'

'Do we have to eat this?' said Sleepy.

As Jenny was about to take her first bite, she could see Uncle Gordon's eyes piercing into her, checking she was going to eat it all up. Jenny took one bite then fell back in her seat, her face despondent.

'Sleepy, I can't eat this. It tastes like castor oil that's gone off,' said Jenny, now looking rather green herself.

Aunty Hilda and Uncle Gordon were making pigs of themselves, tucking into it while the Onion family watched on.

'Time for some fun. I've had enough of this afternoon tea malarkey,' said Sleepy.

'What are you going to do?' asked Jenny. 'You heard what Dad said about being good.'

'Watch this,' replied Sleepy.

Sleepy waved his left paw and Uncle Gordon and Aunty Hilda became frozen in time. Sleepy then waved his right paw and the cake that they were shovelling in like there was no tomorrow levitated just as Uncle Gordon and Aunty Hilda started to move again. As they did so, the next minute, *wham*! The cake split in two, connecting with Uncle Gordon's and Aunty Hilda's face, covering them in cabbage cake.

Harold said, 'I'm so sorry, Gordon and Hilda. I really have no idea how that happened. It must have been some kind of magic. It all happened so fast. Here, let me help you.'

Sleepy whispered to Jenny, 'That's right, it's Sleepy magic,' and the pair of them dissolved into laughter, much to her father's disapproval.

'You must try some of my jelly famous,' Aunty Hilda said, wiping the last of the cake from her face.

'This should be fun,' Jenny said to Sleepy.

'Well hurry up, then,' grunted Uncle Gordon impatiently. He had rather been enjoying that cake and was still rather peckish.

A couple of minutes later Aunty Hilda walked into the room carrying a mountain of wibbly-wobbly red jelly.

Sleepy whispered to Jenny, 'Time to cool off your Uncle Gordon with some jelly.'

The next moment Sleepy waved his left paw and the carpet turned into a mini ski slope. Then *whoosh*! Aunt Hilda slipped and the jelly landed directly on Uncle Gordon's head while Aunty Hilda landed safely on the couch.

'Yes!' Jenny said. 'Great shot, Sleepy.'

'Perhaps now your uncle Gordon won't be so quick ordering people around,' said Sleepy.

Uncle Gordon was covered in cabbage cake and jelly and he was one angry, messy uncle.

'I think it's time we left now,' Harold said promptly. 'Well thank you for the afternoon tea; we must do it again sometime.'

Uncle Gordon looked at him sternly.

'Thank you, Uncle Gordon and Aunty Hilda, that was a lovely afternoon,' Jenny chimed in cheerfully.

Sleepy gave Jenny a big hug as they walked down the garden path.

'You're the best, Sleepy,' said Jenny.

'Thanks, Jenny,' replied Sleepy, giving her a huge hug in return.

Chapter 6

Fun at the Fair

It was the Easter holidays and Jenny had a couple of weeks off school. One bright and breezy Tuesday morning, Jenny and Sleepy were playing in the back garden. Sleepy told Jenny to look over to the sycamore tree and as she did so, out popped Shwizzle, the Easter bunny. Jenny couldn't believe her eyes. Right in front of her was a bunny as white as snow with its ears twizzling around and around.

'Hi there, Shwizzle,' greeted Sleepy.

'Hi to you, too, Sleepy. And hi there, Jenny,' replied Shwizzle. 'Nice to see you again, Sleepy.'

'You know Shwizzle then, Sleepy?' Jenny asked.

'Oh yes. Shwizzle and I always meet up once a year at Easter time, no matter where we are,' replied Sleepy.

'Right, is everyone ready to go to the Easter funfair?' Shwizzle asked them.

'Yes, yes, but I want my mother to come with us on this trip, Sleepy, is that OK?' asked Jenny.

'Of course, that's a sensible idea. I was just about to suggest that myself,' replied Sleepy.

'One minute, Sleepy,' Jenny said and she ran into the kitchen to get her mother. 'Come on, Mum. We're off to the Easter funfair and you are coming with us,' said Jenny.

'Jenny, dear, I'm washing the pots and pans; I have got no time for funfairs,' replied her mother.

'Oh, pleaseee, Mum. Please come with us. You'll enjoy it.'

'Well OK then, Jenny. I'm right behind you.' Mary Onion put on her coat. 'I take it Sleepy is coming with you?'

'Of course he is, Mum, and Shwizzle, too,' replied Jenny.

'Oh no, here we go again. Another Jenny and Sleepy adventure,' Mary said to herself.

Sleepy, Jenny and her mother followed Shwizzle down the path in the back garden until Shwizzle came to a stop by the apple tree.

'Now, can everyone hold hands while I say the magic words,' Shwizzle told the group. 'Flip, flop, flip, flop, open the magic funfair at Castle Hop.'

To Jenny and Mrs Onion's amazement, the back garden disappeared and was transformed into a magical funfair, which looked as big as a city.

'Wow! I can't believe this,' shouted Jenny.

'Come on, everyone, which ride do you want to go on first?' said Shwizzle.

What a choice! The fair was indeed a sight to behold, with hot-air balloons circling in the sky above, roller coasters whizzing round everywhere and not to mention the Sleepster dodgems. Other Easter bunnies were hopping all over the place and all the other children were clutching their own magical bears, but none of them were quite like Jenny's.

'Let's go on the hot-air balloons first, please, Shwizzle.'

'OK, then. Follow me, everyone,' replied Shwizzle as he hopped over towards the ride.

At the entrance to the hot-air balloons an old man in a grey suit and peaked cap said, 'Welcome, Jenny. Welcome, all, to the balloon ride. All aboard.'

Everyone boarded the balloon except Shwizzle, who waved everybody off from the ground.

'Right, just one question. Who is in charge of the controls?' asked Jenny.

'My name is Dutton. I'm your pilot for the trip,' someone or thing said as an umbrella popped out of the locker under the steering wheel. Dutton turned out to be a wooden umbrella with multicoloured fluorescent shapes on it. 'Now, as soon as I press the green button we will take off,' announced Dutton. The next minute the magnificent balloon took off gracefully. 'Now sit back, everyone, and relax. Enjoy the ride.'

Dutton pressed an orange button and a dining table with chairs and a selection of hot foods appeared.

'Yum-yum,' Sleepy and Jenny said together.

'Look! crispy potatoes, sausages, chicken breasts and loads of green vegetables with lots of freshly squeezed fruit juice. Now this is what I call a lunch! Come on, Mum, enjoy – and it saves cooking later,' laughed Jenny.

As everyone tucked into the enormous spread of food the balloon sailed over Tupstall. But Jenny didn't even notice the journey as she was too busy enjoying the food. Lunch passed all too quickly and the balloon was soon readying itself to land back at the funfair at Castle Hop.

'Right, folks, we're about to land,' informed Dutton.

'That was great fun. Come on, Sleepy, let's go,' said an excited Jenny after thanking Dutton and the old man.

'Jenny, I'm so full that even I can't eat another thing, let alone move,' said Mrs Onion.

Shwizzle then popped up as if from nowhere.

'OK, ready for ride two? Let's go, then,' he said, in answer to their eager nods.

Jenny asked Shwizzle if they could go on the Sleepster dodgems next.

'Sure, Jenny. Sleepster dodgems sounds a good choice,' replied Shwizzle.

Everyone followed Shwizzle along the lush green path to the flashing neon dodgems in a huge indoor centre which housed fountains, waterfalls and volcanoes, each erupting with bars of chocolate.

'Wow! these look amazing,' shouted Jenny.

There were ten Sleepster dodgems in all, all in varying colours and all lined up ready to go. Jenny and Sleepy boarded the green one and Shwizzle and Mary took the silver one. Sleepy drove and Jenny did the navigating.

'OK, hold on to your potatoes,' shouted Sleepy as he pressed the white button.

The Sleepster engines roared into life and they took off, closely followed by Shwizzle; Mrs Onion noticeably had her eyes closed firmly. As Shwizzle bumped into Sleepy and Jenny's Sleepster, the huge scoreboard lit up and showed one bump to Shwizzle.

'Right, come on, Sleepy, let's get them!' yelled Jenny.

Sleepy bumped directly into Shwizzle and gained their first point.

'It's the first to reach two points who wins, Jenny,' Sleepy told her.

'Next one wins then, Sleepy,' shouted Jenny hysterically as Shwizzle moved in for the last hit and the winning point.

Sleepy waved his right paw and the dodgem took off in the air and ended up behind Shwizzle. Bump! Sleepy hit the back of Shwizzle's Sleepster.

'We win! We win! That was amazing,' shouted Jenny.

Mary still had her eyes shut.

'Jenny, I've never been so scared in my life but I've had so much fun. Now we must go home, I'm afraid.'

'Well OK, Mum,' said a deflated Jenny.

Shwizzle gave Jenny, Sleepy and Mary a big hug and said, 'See you all next Easter.' Then he told everyone to holds hands before saying the new magic words. 'The fair has been fun, now let me take everyone back to their home without needing to run.'

The next moment Jenny, Mary and Sleepy were all back standing by the apple tree and in their own back garden once again.

'Mum, Sleepy and I are going for a little lie down before dinner.'

'Me too, Jenny, me too,' replied her mother. 'I haven't had so much fun in a long time. The dishes can wait.'

Chapter 7

Mrs McTuddy's Apple Pie Shop

A magnificent dawn greeted the town of Tupstall. Jenny and Sleepy were looking at the birds feeding on the bread that they had left out for them the previous night.

'Listen to the birds, Jenny. They are singing to each other and saying good morning,' said Sleepy.

Jenny listened carefully and she could hear the birds singing what appeared to be, 'Good morning, Jenny.'

'Wow! Sleepy, that's amazing.'

'You should always listen to the birds singing in the morning. They are amazing creatures,' said Sleepy.

Jenny gave Sleepy a big hug in response.

After breakfast Mrs Onion, Jenny and Sleepy drove to Tweedle in the family car for a day out. After an uneventful two-hour journey, during which Sleepy and Jenny played bubble ships, the family arrived at Tweedle, a quaint seaside village with a wide range of antique shops, coffee shops and art galleries.

'Right, you two, let's go shopping,' said Jenny's mother.

As they walked along the cobbled streets Jenny noticed a shop with a sign saying Mrs McTuddy's Apple Pie Shop.

'Mum, please can we go into the apple pie shop? It's Sleepy's favourite dessert; he loves apple pie. Please, Mum, please.'

'Well OK, I suppose we can walk it off when we go shopping afterwards,' replied her mother. 'The sea air always builds up an appetite.'

Sleepy did a little dance to show his approval.

'Yum-yum, apple pie, a very good choice,' a happy Sleepy said.

As they entered the shop they soon realised things weren't normal.

'Jenny, this is no ordinary teashop; I can sense some form of magic here,' said Sleepy.

Jenny and Mrs Onion looked around the teashop and they counted ten mahogany tables and chairs with cutlery and plates laid out on each table. But they weren't plates and cutlery in the normal sense of the words; these ones were talking to each other ...

'Oh look, they've arrived. It's Jenny, Mary and Sleepy,' they said.

'At last,' one of the plates replied.

Around the walls were paintings of people sitting down eating apple pies, only to be replaced once they had finished them, like never-ending pies. In the middle of the room was a wishing well with a sign saying:

Welcome to the wishing well of answers. Please throw a penny in to find out your answer to the question.

Mrs Onion, Jenny and Sleepy sat down at a table and realised no other customers were in the teashop. A little old lady appeared out of nowhere, dressed in a shawl and tweed skirt. She spoke softly to them in a Scottish accent.

'Hello, you three. I have been expecting you. I'm Mrs McTuddy, the owner of McTuddy's Apple Pie Shop. Right, then, if you're ready I'll take your order.'

Jenny opened the menu, which began to speak to them.

'Hello, I'm Pudd, your menu for today. Can I recommend McTuddy's apple pie with extra ice cream?'

Sleepy nearly passed out on hearing that.

'Yes, let's take that. Thanks, Pudd,' replied Sleepy.

While everybody was waiting for the food, which Mrs McTuddy had gone to prepare, the cutlery began chatting to Sleepy.

'Well, Sleepy, how are you keeping?' asked Silver, the talking fork.

'I'm fine, Silver,' replied Sleepy.

'I hope you are behaving yourself, Sleepy,' said Silver.

'Always,' replied Sleepy with a wink at Jenny.

Just then, Mrs McTuddy brought out three enormous portions of hot apple pie with ice cream.

'Enjoy, everybody, I know you will,' she said.

They each began to tuck into the dessert.

'Wow! This apple pie's amazing. I can't believe it,' said Jenny.

'Yes, it's simply splendid,' her mother agreed.

Sleepy just ate and ate, saying nothing but doing a little dance with his paws after each mouthful. Every plate was completely clean and everyone was full.

'Thank you, Mrs McTuddy, that was the best apple pie we have ever had,' said Jenny.

'You are most welcome. I told you that you would enjoy it.'

Mrs Onion said, 'Please would you pay Mrs McTuddy, Sleepy? Here's some money.'

Sleepy paid Mrs McTuddy and she gave him a penny change. He then threw the penny into the wishing well. Kerplunk! The penny sank to the bottom of the well and Sleepy closed his eyes, made a wish then went back to the table.

'All settled,' he said. 'Let's go shopping now.'

On their way out of the teashop, Mrs McTuddy whispered something into Sleepy's ear. Sleepy replied by simply nodding to her.

'Goodbye, Mrs McTuddy. See you again,' Jenny said.

'Thank you, Jenny, I'm sure you will somewhere,' replied Mrs McTuddy, closing the teashop door behind them.

Mrs Onion bought her husband a fishing rod for £40 at a nearby shop as a birthday present. As they began walking towards the car, Jenny noticed that Mrs McTuddy's Apple Pie Shop had disappeared.

'Mum, Mum, it's gone, the apple pie shop has gone. Look! There's just a brick wall there now.'

'It's crazy but you are right, it has gone,' she replied.

'Don't worry, Jenny,' said Sleepy. 'I'll explain it all later.'

'Thanks, Sleepy,' replied a curious Jenny.

Chapter 8

Sleepy Mountain

That night Jenny and Sleepy were playing with Jenny's train set Choo-Choo in her bedroom, when Jenny asked Sleepy about what had happened earlier in the day.

'I'm worried about what happened to Mrs McTuddy's Apple Pie Shop,' she explained. 'How did it just vanish? Please tell me, Sleepy.'

'Mrs McTuddy is not from this world. She is from my world, Magicville. Mrs McTuddy was sent by my king, King Magic, with a very important message to give to me. My friends Cuff Cuff and Sunshine have been captured by Pirate Penguin. It's important they are rescued as my world's existence depends on it.

'The only way back to Magicville is by going through the magic waterfall at Sleepy Mountain. When I threw that penny in the wishing well at Mrs McTuddy's shop, that's what I wished for – information – as I knew there was a problem in Magicville.'

'Can I come with you, Sleepy?' asked Jenny.

'You can, but to stop your parents worrying about you when you are away, I'll have to freeze them in time here,

so they won't know you have even been away. When we come back it will be a few hours later from when we left,' said Sleepy, 'but to them no time will have passed at all.'

The next morning Jenny and Sleepy were ready to head off to Sleepy Mountain.

'OK, Sleepy, let's go,' urged an impatient Jenny. 'Mum, Sleepy and I are off out to play.'

'OK,' her mother replied as she was doing the washing-up.

Sleepy waved his left paw and Mrs Onion became frozen in time, holding the plate above the washing-up bowl. Then her father, Harold, who was busy mowing the grass, froze when Sleepy shook his left paw.

'Don't worry; they are both fine, Jenny, and you will see them soon.'

Sleepy waved his right paw and the sound of the Sleepsters' engines could be heard roaring round to the front of the house.

'Well, if you are ready, Jenny, then let the adventure begin,' said Sleepy.

'Let's go, Sleepy,' replied Jenny excitedly as they boarded the Sleepster.

'Hold on tight, Jenny, we're off to Sleepy Mountain,' said Sleepy.

Sleepy pressed the blue button on the Sleepsters' dashboard and like a bolt of lightning, it set off for Sleepy Mountain.

'We will be there soon, Jenny, enjoy the ride,' Sleepy said.

Jenny was used to being a passenger in the Sleepster by now and after the car had weaved its way through the traffic, they were soon out of the city and heading towards the rolling hills of the Tupstall countryside. Higher and higher the Sleepster climbed, and louder and louder the engines roared.

'Sleepy, we're nearly in the clouds,' said Jenny.

'Don't worry, Jenny, not far now.'

Jenny soon saw a sign on top of a wooden bridge saying "Welcome to Sleepy Mountain".

'We're here, Jenny. Just over this bridge you will see Sleepy Mountain.'

They drove over the stone bridge and everything suddenly changed. The grass was no longer green but orange and the sky was pink. Directly ahead of them was a magnificent sight, with a waterfall which rather than flowing down vertically instead went in a sort of criss-cross pattern, catching the sunlight in a rainbow of colours. Shiny rocks were embedded all around it.

'There is no time to lose,' said Sleepy. 'When I place my paw on the rock by the waterfall we will be transported to Magicville through the magic time hole. OK, here we go, Jenny. Hold on to me, there's nothing to be afraid of.'

Jenny held on tight to Sleepy's waist while the bear placed his right paw on the rock. But nothing happened.

'Oh no, Jenny, we can't get through the magic time hole.'

'Why not, Sleepy?' asked a concerned Jenny.

A message from the rock landed on Sleepy's paw which read:

Sleepy, the only way to get through the magic time hole is for you to find the Key of Time.

The note then burst into flames.

'Jenny, the only person who knows where the Key of Time is now is Professor Pear.'

'Who is Professor Pear?'

'He is a very wise man, Jenny. He is 980 years of age and he lives in a village called Peardrop. We must leave now for Professor Pear's home before it's too late,' urged Sleepy.

Jenny and Sleepy quickly climbed aboard the Sleepster and the car roared off over the bridge towards the village of Peardrop.

'It will only take us three minutes to travel the 200 miles to Professor Pear's home, Jenny. Hold on while I press the green button.'

Sleepy pressed the green button and the Sleepster began to hover before flying faster than any bird or aeroplane in the sky she had ever seen. Whoosh!

'Sleepy, this is unbelievable!' said Jenny.

'We are nearly there now, Jenny. Hold on. Just a couple more minutes,' said Sleepy.

The Sleepster landed in the village of Peardrop moments later.

'This is Professor Pear's house,' Sleepy told Jenny.

'Wow! what a strange-looking house. I've never seen a house like this in my entire life,' said a confused Jenny.

Chapter 9

The Wonderful Professor Pear

Professor Pear's home was like no other house in Peardrop. First of all it was in the shape of a huge pear, with a moat running all around the little house. Small boats were meandering around the moat, all in the shape of pears.

'Are you sure Professor Pear can help, Sleepy?' asked Jenny. 'This looks like a really odd house.'

'Don't worry, we are in the best place if we are to get any help,' replied Sleepy.

Jenny and Sleepy boarded one of the larger pear boats and a sail appeared, also in the shape of a pear. Before they knew it, Jenny and Sleepy were at the front door of Professor Pear's house. Sleepy rang the doorbell and a "bing-bang-bong" sound was emitted.

The door opened almost immediately and an elderly man wearing a gold coloured waistcoat and dark trousers with a white beard and a head in the shape of the pear greeted the pair of them.

'I've been expecting you. Please, follow me to my library. There is lots to discuss and not a moment to lose,' stated the Professor.

On the way to the library Jenny saw a variety of pictures on the wall, all seemingly of Professor Pear's family through the generations. Jenny noticed that the pictures were winking at her. She also saw several suits of armour standing in a line, almost as if to attention. One of the hands in the suits waved at Jenny as she entered the library. Jenny thought how odd it was to have suits of armour that moved.

As they sat down Professor Pear said, 'I understand you need to find the Key of Time to get to Magicville, Sleepy. My sources tell me that the magic waterfall wouldn't let you through at Sleepy Mountain.'

'That is correct,' affirmed Sleepy.

'I see,' said the Professor as he stroked his white beard. 'Now, to find the Key of Time you must go to Cave Island where the key is now located. I cannot tell you exactly where, but you will find it in one of the many secret caves.

'Beware, though, for you will have to travel across Rocky Road. To help you pass Rocky Road in safety, please take this magic flute with you; it will help you on your journey. You must use it whenever you face any dangers.

'Once you have found the Key of Time you will then be able to get through the magic time hole at Sleepy Mountain. But please be quick as Cuff Cuff and Sunshine are in deep danger,' stated the Professor.

'Thank you, Professor Pear,' replied Sleepy. 'We will do what we can.'

Jenny and Sleepy both gave Professor Pear a big hug before making their way to the front door of his pear shaped house. Once again, the suit of armour waved to Jenny before they climbed into the pear sail boat and made their way back to the Sleepster.

They jumped into the Sleepster and Sleepy started the engines. The Sleepster then roared off into the distance. Jenny and Sleepy caught sight of the blurred form of Professor Pear waving to them as they left the village of Pear drop.

'Professor Pear seemed nice,' said Jenny.

'Yes, he's a very nice and a very wise man who has given us the important information we needed,' replied Sleepy.

'Do you think we might meet him again?'

'We may very well do.'

'Sleepy, what does that sign say ahead of us?' said a worried Jenny urgently.

Sleepy read out the sign which said:

Danger – you are about to enter Rocky Road.

Chapter 10

Hold on Tight

Sleepy slowed the Sleepster down as it approached Rocky Road. Ahead of them was what seemed a very wide road with huge boulders stacked to the edge of either side of the road with huge cliffs rising behind them.

'Jenny, this is going to be very dangerous. Hold on tight and try not to be scared,' said Sleepy.

'OK, Sleepy, whatever you say,' replied Jenny.

The Sleepster moved forwards slowly and the engines sounded a lot quieter than normal. Jenny then felt the road move and shake beneath them.

'Oh no! Sleepy, what's happening? Help!'

'Don't worry, Jenny,' said Sleepy as the road started to tilt, 'just keep holding on tight.'

Sleepy fought hard to keep the Sleepster from turning upside down. More boulders on each of the cliffs began to crash down on the road, just missing the Sleepster. It required all of Sleepy's driving skills to avoid them.

Crash! Another boulder landed on the road, this time catching the Sleepsters' headlight.

'It's OK, Jenny, we're OK,' Sleepy shouted. Just then, Sleepy remembered the flute. 'Jenny, the flute! Play the magic flute Professor Pear gave you.'

Jenny did as Sleepy asked and immediately, straight out of the earth emerged hundreds of huge oak trees. They appeared as if from nowhere and all were over 100 feet high. As the boulders continued to crash down all around them the trees stopped them from landing on the Sleepster.

'Yippee! we are safe,' shouted Jenny. Then she saw a sign saying: "Well done! You have safely passed Rocky Road". 'I don't want to go back that way, Sleepy. Must we go back that way?'

'Don't worry, Jenny, I'll make sure we don't have to. It's a good job we had Professor Pear's magical flute. Now it's off to Cave Island,' said Sleepy.

Just then, Sleepy saw masses of flying geese in the sky.

'Look! Jenny, look at the geese – they will show us the way to Cave Island.'

Jenny watched the geese and sure enough, they flew in a pattern in the shape of an arrow. All Sleepy had to do was to follow the arrow in the sky. Minutes later, the Sleepster arrived near Cave Island. To reach the island itself they had to cross a large section of choppy water.

'Any ideas how we get across the water?' asked Jenny.

'Yes, I have as a matter of fact. Use the flute again,' replied Sleepy.

Jenny started to play the flute and a loud rumbling sound came from the direction of the water, out of which emerged a huge hippopotamus. Jenny took a few steps back in shock. It wasn't just that it was a hippopotamus, it was the fact that it was talking. But there again, what with everything else that had happened since she had known Sleepy, she should hardly have been surprised.

'Hi, I'm Happy Hippo, your ferry ride to Cave Island. All aboard.'

Sleepy and Jenny jumped on the back of Happy Hippo and off they went to Cave Island.

'Why are you called Happy?' asked Jenny as the waves crashed all around them.

'Oh! that's easy. It's because I'm always singing happy tunes,' replied Happy, immediately starting to live up to his name. 'I'm happy, so happy, and that's why they call me Happy Hippo. I'm happy, so happy, the Happy Hippo.'

Happy Hippo continued singing throughout the relatively short journey.

'I see now why you are called Happy,' said Jenny, 'thank you.'

'It's my pleasure to have helped you. Right, Sleepy, Jenny, welcome to Cave Island. To find the Key of Time you need to get to the Cave of Flumes, which is located a mile to the east,' said Happy.

'Thanks, Happy,' replied Jenny.

'How do we call you when we're ready for a ride back?' asked Sleepy.

'No problem, I'll be listening out for you. Just play the magical flute again,' replied Happy as she dived under the water resuming her song.

Jenny and Sleepy passed cave after cave as they travelled east until they came across the Cave of Flumes with swirling water and logs around it.

'Right, Sleepy, let's jump on a log and it will take us into the cave with the movement of the current.'

Sleepy and Jenny jumped onto the log and they floated slowly into the Cave of Flumes. The cave was very dark indeed and surprisingly warm. Then a loud voice came from the ceiling of the cave, startling them.

'Welcome, Jenny and Sleepy. I'm Finkle and I'll guide you to the Key of Time. Please listen carefully to my instructions.'

'We will,' replied Jenny.

The log gathered pace, going faster and faster, zooming around the corners, soaking the pair of them. Then the log stopped abruptly with a huge spray of water.

'You can get off now,' said Finkle. 'Make sure you take the left passage, Sleepy, and don't let anyone or thing tell you otherwise.'

Sleepy and Jenny started to run down the left passage.

'Stop!' shouted Sleepy. There was a huge hole just a further ten steps away with a 1,000 feet drop. 'Hold on to me, Jenny, and I will make sure we get across safely.'

Sleepy waved his left paw and the pair of them began to hover in mid-air.

'Wow, Sleepy, you can fly,' said Jenny, astonished.

'Yes, my magic allows me to fly as well.'

Sleepy and Jenny landed safely on the other side of the hole. Jenny then saw some markings on the wall of the cave in the shape of a castle and a ship.

'Behind this wall lies the Key of Time,' said Sleepy.

Putting his right paw on the wall, it opened up in different segments. There in a section of the wall lay the Key of Time.

'We've done it, Sleepy. Let's get the key and get out of here,' shouted Jenny.

Sleepy grabbed the key in it and they headed back through the passage to the log, flying over the hole that they came across last time.

As they jumped on the log, Finkle said, 'Well done, you two. Now quickly. You must leave the Cave of Flumes. And good luck.'

'Thank you, Finkle,' replied Jenny.

The two of them jumped off the log and then headed to the other side of Cave Island. They stopped at the edge of the water, where Jenny played on the magical flute, and out came Happy Hippo.

'Hi, you two. Did you manage to locate the Key of Time?'

'Yes, we did, Happy, we have it right here,' replied Sleepy.

'Well done, you two. Then I guess it's all aboard again,' said Happy, who immediately began swimming while singing his favourite song.

Sleepy and Jenny hugged each other while the waves crashed around them, not caring how soaked they both got.

'I'm so glad we have the Key of Time, Sleepy. I just hope it works.'

'Me, too, Jenny. Now all that's left to do is to get to Sleepy Mountain as fast as we can. Cuff Cuff and Sunshine need our help and quickly,' said Sleepy.

Jenny and Sleepy climbed off Happy.

'Thank you so much, Happy; you have been a great help,' said Sleepy.

'Always a pleasure,' replied Happy.

Happy then dived under the water, soaking Sleepy and Jenny some more as she disappeared beneath the surface.

Chapter 11

The Key of Time

Sleepy and Jenny jumped into the Sleepster.

'Jenny, we need to move fast; we have to get to Sleepy Mountain as quickly as possible,' said Sleepy.

'Please tell me we aren't going via Rocky Road again, Sleepy,' said a now worried Jenny.

'Have no fear; I know a short-cut,' replied Sleepy.

Sleepy pressed the pink button on the Sleepsters' dashboard and the car began to take off. After about ten minutes they were nearing Sleepy Mountain. Suddenly, Jenny could hear what sounded like a horse galloping in the distance.

'Sleepy, can you hear the sound of a horse?' asked Jenny.

'Yes, I can. It's Chestnut; he's trying to catch up with us. I'll slow down,' replied Sleepy.

Sleepy pressed the brakes on the Sleepster and while they were still in mid-air, they were now travelling at only half their previous speed. Chestnut the flying horse was soon alongside the Sleepster. Chestnut was a friendly giant of a horse with magnificent graceful features.

'Hi, Chestnut. What brings you over this way?' asked Sleepy.

'I have a message from Cuff Cuff and Sunshine, Sleepy. Things are a lot worse than they seem. Pirate Penguin has them locked in his dungeon on board his ship, *The Slippery Snake*, and I fear they are very close to telling him the magic secret,' said Chestnut.

'Thank you, Chestnut. Can you fly back and tell King Magic I'm on my way with Jenny to see him at the magical palace. We will rescue Cuff Cuff and Sunshine soon enough, so don't you worry,' said Sleepy.

'I'm on my way now. Goodbye, Sleepy. Goodbye, Jenny.'

Chestnut flew into the distance as Jenny and Sleepy waved goodbye to him and soon he was out of sight.

'Sleepy, who is this Pirate Penguin and why did he capture Cuff Cuff and Sunshine?' asked Jenny.

'Pirate Penguin is half bear and half penguin. He is after the secret to our magic powers. He wants to use the powers for himself and for his crab army so he can take over Magicville.

'He believes Cuff Cuff and Sunshine know the magic formula as they were at the School of Magic where the magic was created. King Magic and I have been trying to find Pirate Penguin for many years but he keeps escaping,' said Sleepy.

'I understand now, Sleepy,' replied Jenny.

'Jenny, we are approaching Sleepy Mountain, now do you have the Key of Time?' asked Sleepy.

'Yes, I have it here in my hand.'

'OK, hold on tight while I land the Sleepster, Jenny.'

Sleepy brought the car down next to the magic waterfall and the two of them jumped out and headed over to the rock by the magic waterfall. Sleepy placed the Key of Time on the rock.

'Well, here goes, Jenny. When I wave my paw the rock will open and we should be greeted by Snorkel, the gatekeeper of the time hole at Magicville. Hold on to my waist and whatever you do, please do not let go of me,' said Sleepy.

'No problem, Sleepy,' replied Jenny, now a little anxious as she put her arms around his waist.

'OK, here goes.'

Sleepy waved his left paw and the rocks opened up, sucking Sleepy and Jenny into the magic time hole.

'Are you OK?' asked Sleepy.

'I'm fine. I can see Earth behind us, Sleepy,' replied Jenny.

'We are travelling at 450 million miles per hour. Don't worry about the bolts of lightning; it's perfectly normal. Snorkel is guiding us to Magicville Airport.'

All of a sudden, Sleepy and Jenny landed right in the middle of the departure lounge. Ahead of them a sign said:

Welcome to Magicville Airport. Please go to Gate Three if you have the Key of Time on you.

'Wow!' said Jenny suddenly. 'Look at the sky; it's all purple. And just look at that, Sleepy. What on earth is it?'

'It's the flying elephant planes we have here called snorks. They are always busy taking off and landing. They travel to destinations all around Magicville,' explained Sleepy.

Jenny saw eight huge flying elephants, all of different colours, taking off and landing in succession.

'Now, Jenny, we need to get to Gate Three; Snorkel will be there to meet us.'

They began to make their way to Gate Three. The airport was very busy and was full of hundreds of passengers including bears, rabbits, giraffes and zebras.

'Look, Sleepy, there it is, gate number three,' said Jenny.

The two of them ran to the gate and from behind a desk up popped Snorkel, the elephant. Snorkel had his round glasses on and was an unmistakeable pink colour. He was drinking from a nearby fountain with his extra-long trunk.

'Sleepy, Jenny, it's so good to see you both. I hope the journey through the magic time hole was smooth.'

'Look at the *Magicville Chronicle* newspaper, Jenny. It's all about Pirate Penguin.' Said Sleepy

'Everybody is very worried,' said Snorkel. 'I must get you both to King Magic now; he is waiting for you and there is no time to be lost. Follow me through the green door; I have a nice surprise for you to get you to the palace quicker that I think young Jenny here may find rather interesting.'

Sleepy knew what the surprise was but he did not want to spoil it for Jenny.

'Look! Sleepy, it's the Sleepster,' she exclaimed.

Sleepy and Jenny gave Snorkel a hug while the Sleepsters' engines were fired up. Then Sleepy pressed the green button this time and the Sleepster took off into the purple sky. Sleepy weaved the car past the snorks and other Sleepsters and headed towards the Palace of King Magic ...

Chapter 12

The Palace of King Magic

In the distance Jenny and Sleepy could see the Palace of King Magic getting bigger as they drew nearer and nearer.

'Look at that, Sleepy. It's the most amazing palace I have ever seen – a palace fit for any king,' shouted Jenny above the roar of the engines.

The palace was a huge stunning building which seemed to go on and on. It truly was an exceptional sight. Sleepy and Jenny were greeted by a group pelicans who were now flying next to the Sleepster. The pelicans were all of various shades of blue, green and orange. The lead pelican called Pel instructed Sleepy to guide the Sleepster to the royal courtyard.

'Please follow me, Sleepy. We have your landing space ready,' stated Pel.

Sleepy landed the car safely in the royal courtyard. They were then escorted by four royal guards dressed in smart green uniforms with the crest of King Magic on their shields. The guards were much larger bears than Sleepy, but Sleepy knew they were on his side and so they followed without fear.

One of the guards called Dwink said, 'You must follow us to the royal observation tower. King Magic is waiting for you.'

Jenny and Sleepy walked briskly through the palace behind the bear guards and as they did so, they noticed that the floor pattern kept changing colour. Looking up, they saw that the ceilings had fountains on them with water somehow flowing from them, yet not a drop landed on the floor.

The royal guards stopped outside a large oak door and knocked three times. The door opened and there stood King Magic. He was a sight to behold with his royal robe and crown, all made from the finest materials. He was slightly taller than Sleepy and he had a friendly, kind face. King Magic spoke in a concerned but clear voice.

'Welcome, Jenny. Welcome, Sleepy. Thank you for coming so quickly. I understand from Professor Pear that you had to locate the Key of Time in order to get through the time hole. You have both done well and you should be congratulated for your efforts.'

Sleepy winked at Jenny.

'Come, we have work to do. As you know, Pirate Penguin has captured our dear friends Cuff Cuff and Sunshine. He believes they know the secret to our magic powers and sadly, he is correct. I can confirm that Sunshine and Cuff Cuff do indeed know the secret formula as they were there, when Professor Triangle created the magical powers more than 9,000 years ago.

'If Pirate Penguin gets hold of the formula he will use the magic to take over the land with his army of crabs and nothing will be able to stop him. I know that with your magical powers, Sleepy, and your courage, Jenny, you can rescue Cuff Cuff and Sunshine and capture Pirate Penguin,' said King Magic.

The King moved to the royal telescope and said, 'Pirate Penguin is keeping Cuff Cuff and Sunshine prisoners on board his ship just off Crab Island.'

'Did you say Crab Island, Your Majesty?' replied Sleepy.

'I'm afraid so, Sleepy. This means the journey will be a dangerous one and you will meet many obstacles along your way. To help you on your journey, please take these two items with you. For you, Jenny, I have here a magical watch. Keep it on you at all times. When you press the gold button, the watch will generate a shield around you that will last for thirty seconds, during which nothing can hurt you in any way.

'For you, Sleepy, there is no magic I can give you as you have everything you need to keep you safe. All except the map of Tronja, that is. This map will guide you to Crab Island. Now please let us hug as we do in our land, to wish you luck and a safe journey.

'Sleepy, Jenny, the Kingdom of Magicville is in your hands now. I know you will do your best,' said King Magic.

'Don't worry, Your Majesty, we will succeed in our mission,' replied Sleepy.

As Sleepy and Jenny began walking out of the observatory, King Magic took another look through the telescope then shook his head in a worried manner. Together, they made their way back through the palace towards the Sleepster.

'Well, Jenny, here we go. Are you ready to save Cuff Cuff, Sunshine and everyone in Magicville?'

Jenny gave Sleepy a big hug and said, 'Yes, I know we will do it, Sleepy. I trust you and I love you with all my heart. We will find Cuff Cuff and Sunshine come what may. Let's go.'

Sleepy knew Jenny meant every word that he said and he told her that he loved her, too. Sleepy then fired up the Sleepsters' engines and they took off once again into the purple sky. In the distance they could see King Magic waving to them from the observatory and Jenny and Sleepy knew their new adventure was only just about to begin ...

More Adventures coming soon …

Rescue in Magicville

The 3 Silver Coins